Get the Fruit!

Written by Paul Shipton
Illustrated by Trevor Dunton

Collins

2

3

9

14

15

Ideas for guided reading

Learning objectives: to understand and use correctly terms about books and print; to be aware of story structures; to make collections of new words linked to own interest, topics; to explore animal and jungle sounds using instruments and voice

Curriculum links: Mathematical development: Use ideas to solve practical problems

Getting started

- Look at the book together and point out the cover, title, pictures, beginning and end. Discuss what is on the cover – *monkeys, fruit tree*. Ask what the monkeys are thinking. Then read the title to see if the children are right.

- Model the process of turning to the title page. Prompt the children to look closely at the fruit in the illustration and suggest words to describe it, e.g. *green, tasty, yummy,* etc.

- Walk through the book and model how to tell the story in your own words, using story language. Stop at p9 and ask what the monkeys are thinking – what is their plan?

Reading and responding

- Ask the children to tell the story up to p13 to a partner. Prompt the children to use story language, and to look at the pictures carefully before turning the page in order to make predictions. Observe the children's page turning and left-right scanning, intervening if necessary.

- Prompt and praise their use of interesting and new words as the children talk through the pictures. Write these on a whiteboard.

- Prompt and praise the children's predictions. They could connect them to their own experiences, e.g. *When I couldn't reach the table, I climbed up on Mum's chair.*